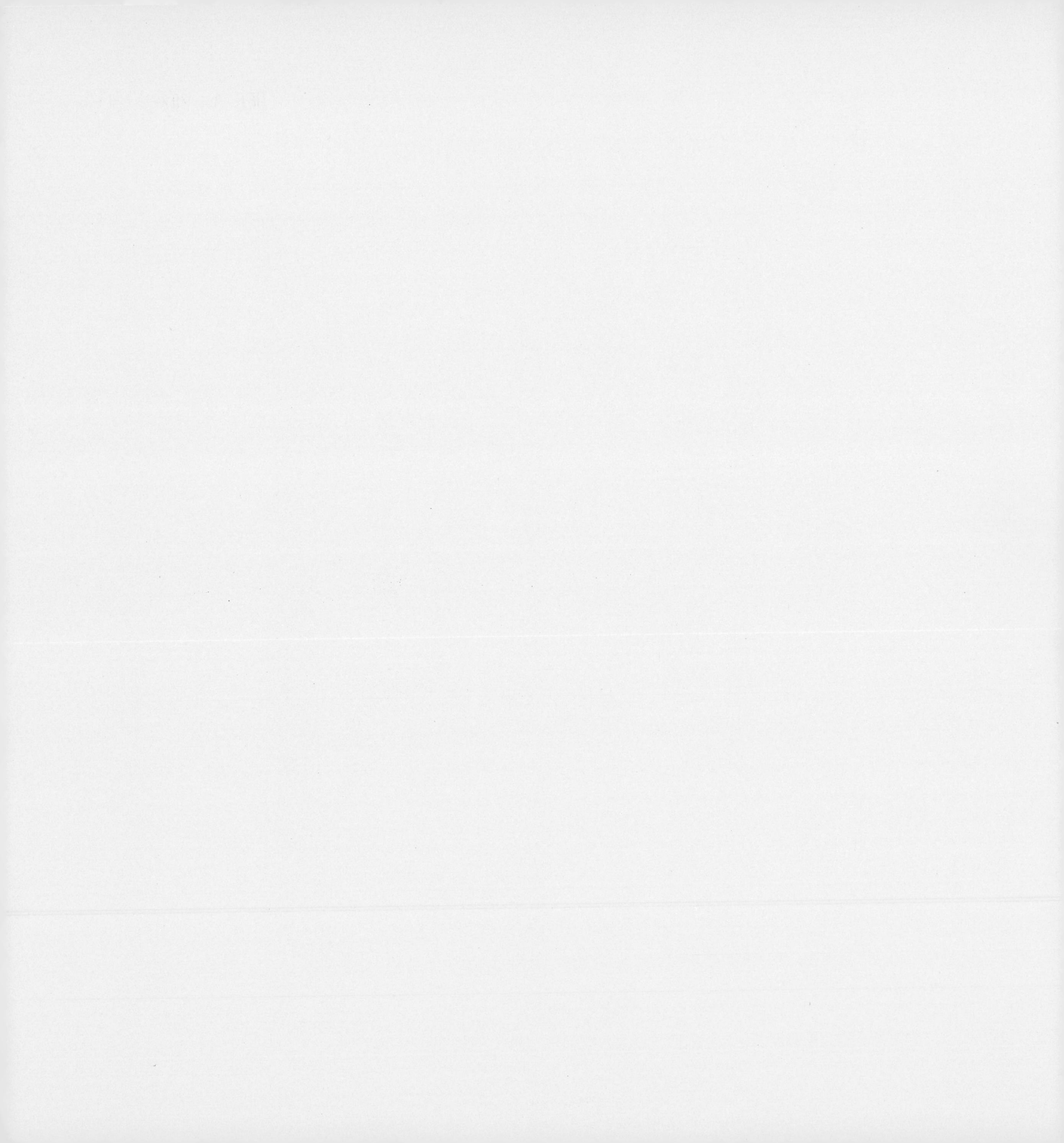

written by *New York Times*–bestselling author
Beth Ferry

illustrated by Caldecott Honor winner
Molly Idle

Roaring Brook Press
New York

We believe
in climbing higher.

We believe in digging deep.

We believe in drinking sunshine.

We believe in beauty sleep.

We believe in making music.
We believe in singing loud.

We believe in being funny.

WE BELIEVE IN

BEING WOWED.

We believe
in exploration.

We believe in
standing tall.

We believe in having courage.

We believe that life's a ball!

We believe in helping others.

We believe in shining light.

We believe in making memories.

We believe we're out of sight!

We believe in slow and steady.

We believe in families.

We believe in peaceful living.

WE BELIEVE THE

WORLD NEEDS TREES.

We believe in lots of hugging.

We believe that groups are smart.

We believe in smacks of sweetness.

WE
BELIEVE
WE'RE

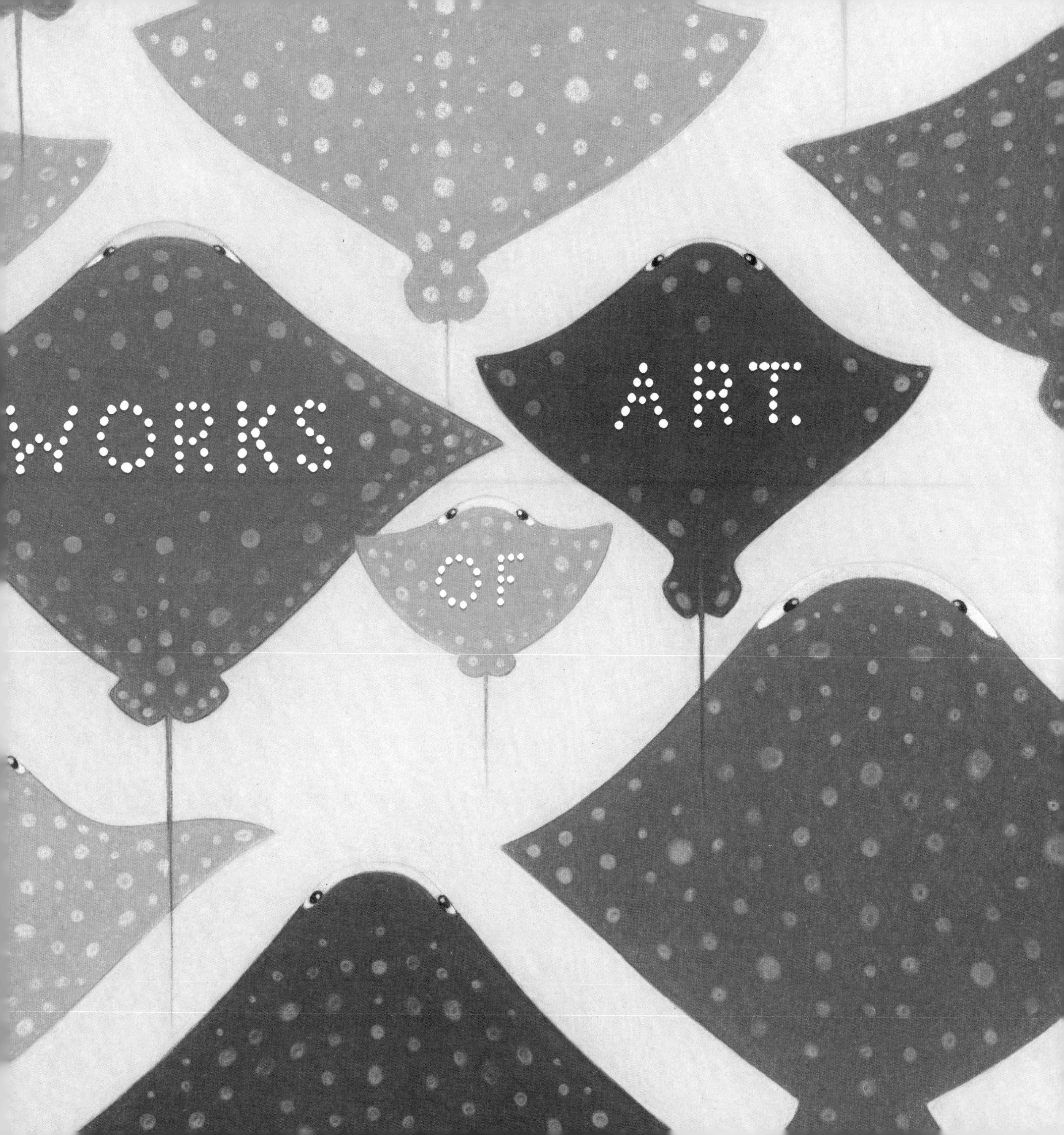
WORKS
ART.
OF

We believe in working harder.

We believe in playing more.

We believe that life's a journey.
We believe it's time . . .

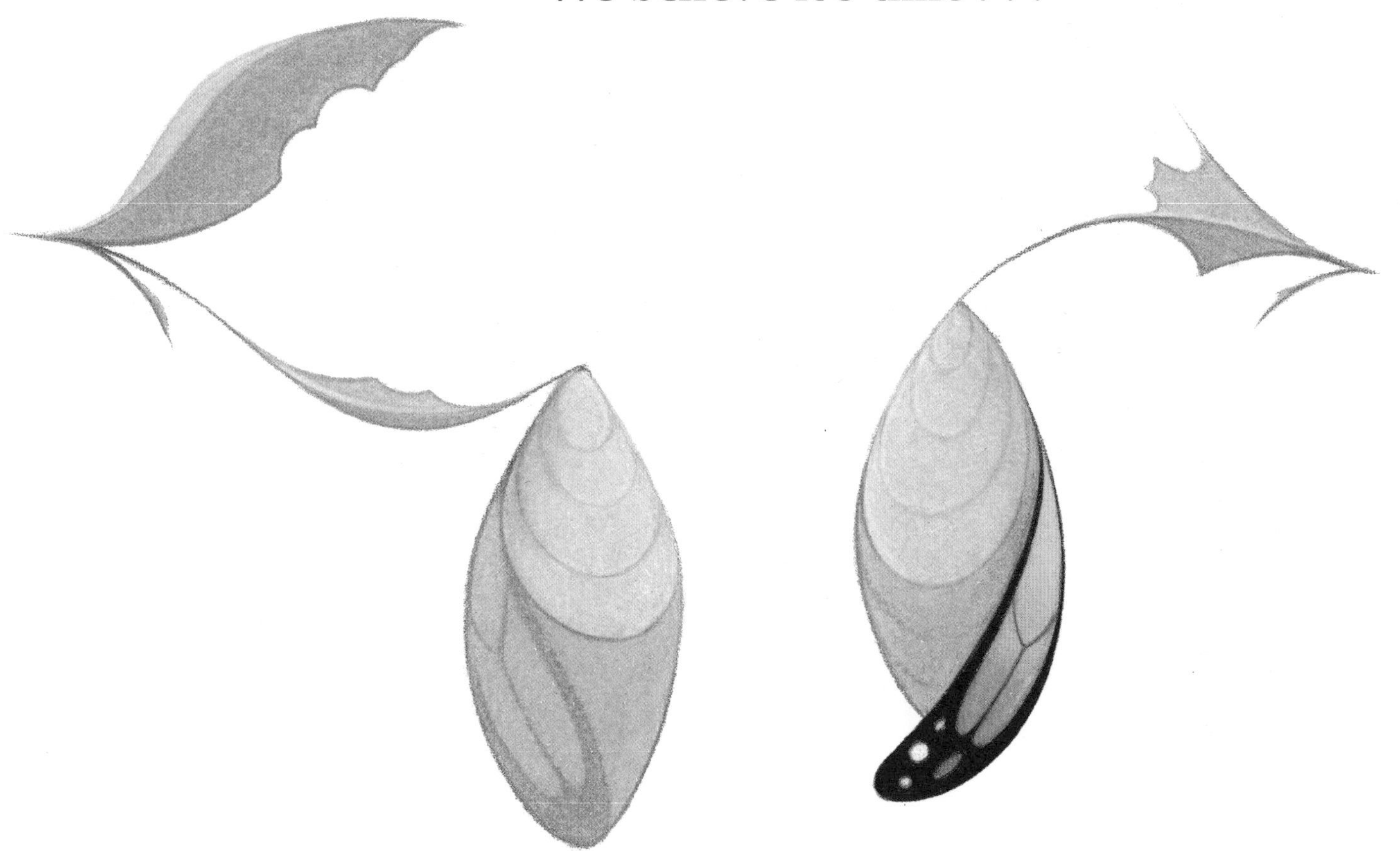

. . . to SOAR!

Do you believe
in happy endings?

Do you believe
that dreams come true?

We believe it. Absolutely!

Just like . . .

WE BELIEVE IN YOU.

For Elena, agent extraordinaire,

who has always believed in me.

—B.F.

For Mom and Dad,

who believed in me from the very start.

—M.I.

Published by Roaring Brook Press • Roaring Brook Press

is a division of Holtzbrinck Publishing Holdings Limited Partnership

120 Broadway, New York, NY 10271 • mackids.com •

Library of Congress Cataloging-in-Publication Data is available • ISBN 978-1-250-31200-6

Our books may be purchased in bulk for promotional, educational, or business use.

Please contact your local bookseller or the Macmillan Corporate and Premium Sales Department

at (800) 221-7945 ext. 5442 or by email at MacmillanSpecialMarkets@macmillan.com • First edition, 2020 • Book design

by Jen Keenan • Printed in China by Hung Hing Off-set Printing Co. Ltd., Heshan City, Guangdong Province • 10 9 8 7 6 5 4 3 2 1